The Night Library

by David Zeltser   *illustrated by* Raul Colón

Random House 🏠 New York

It was the night before my eighth birthday, and I was having trouble falling asleep. A thick blanket of snow had silenced the streets outside. I could hear my parents' whispers in the hallway. I heard footsteps approaching, and my door opened.

"Would you like your present now?" asked my father.

"Really?" I said excitedly. "What is it?"

"A book," said my mother. "I thought we could read it together."

I stared at it. "A *book*?" I said, frowning.

I couldn't understand it. My parents knew that I liked toys, games, and movies—not books.

After they left, I fell into a restless sleep.

In the middle of the night, I was awoken by a strange sound coming from outside. It sounded like a deep purring.

When I peeked through the window, I almost fell out of bed. There was a lion on the lawn, looking up at me. I thought it might be a statue until I saw the enormous paw prints in the snow. The lion purred again.

It was a welcoming sound, and I soon found myself outside.

"Climb on," said the lion in a deep, gentle voice.

"Where are we going?" I asked.

"We are going to meet Patience," he said. "I am Fortitude."

The lion looked oddly familiar.

Fortitude whisked me silently across our snow-covered
street. The wind whistled in my ears as we picked up speed.
We raced through Woodlawn Cemetery and past Yankee
Stadium. We sped along the moonlit river toward the
skyscrapers of Manhattan. Eventually, we turned onto
41st Street, entering the heart of the frozen city.

We finally stopped in front of a huge marble building. It had arched windows and three bronze doors—all shut tight. Carved across the top of the edifice were the words *The New York Public Library.*

"The library?" I said. "You brought me to a library in the middle of the night?"

Fortitude turned and regarded me, eyes twinkling. One of the doors swung silently open, and a light flickered on. The lion carried me inside.

Fortitude bounded up the steps of the grand hall. He carried me into a magnificent room with dozens of long, empty tables. Most impressive of all were the towering shelves holding countless books.

We seemed to be alone, but I heard a strange humming sound coming from the shelves.

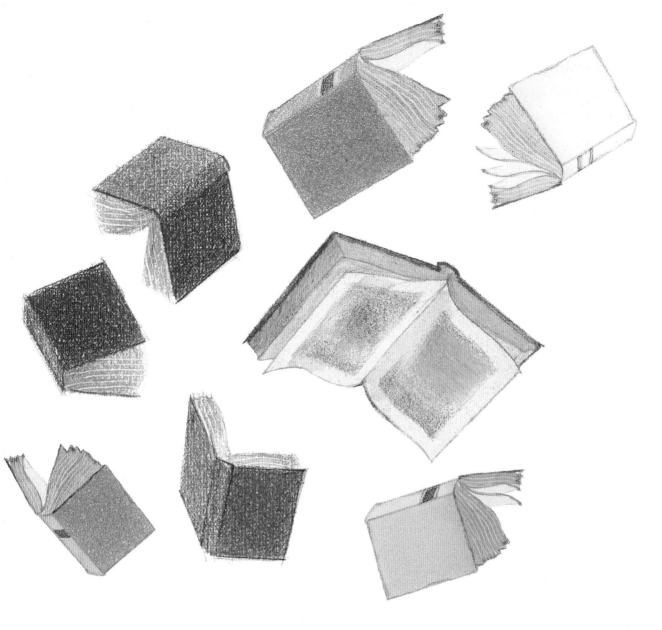

I peered at some of the books up close. They were moving! Some jittered, others swayed, a few twirled gracefully.

I reached for a book, but it jumped out of my hand. I laughed as another skittered away from me.

"Adult books can be difficult to grasp," said the lion. "Let's go to the children's section."

"Am I dreaming?" I asked as he carried me down the staircase.

In the children's section, the books were much more playful. Every chair was a ladder and every table a stage. A jumble of books had arranged themselves to form a rabbit—dashing away from another pile shaped like a man carrying a rake.

"That's Peter Rabbit and Mr. McGregor!" I blurted out. My grandpa had read *The Tale of Peter Rabbit* to me dozens of times when I was little.

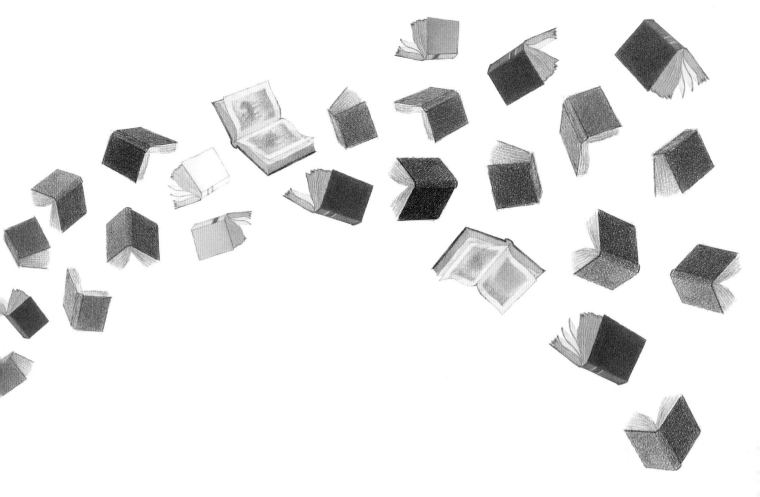

"And they're playing *The Cat in the Hat*!" I cried. "My grandpa taught me to read with that story."

A whistle sounded, and a train made entirely of books chugged through the room.

"The Polar Express," I whispered to the lion. "My grandpa and I used to read that together every Christmas."

"Why did you stop?" asked Fortitude.

"My grandpa died."

Suddenly, the books dropped their games and began to form something new.

The books came together into the shape of my grandpa and me in his favorite chair, reading together.

As Fortitude watched, I reached out and touched the figure of my grandpa. I gasped as I saw that these were the very books he had once read to me.

"Looks like you found your books," said a voice just behind me.

I turned to face another lion.
"I am Patience," he said in a quiet, strong voice.
I looked from him to the figure of my grandpa.
"Those books have been waiting for you," said Patience.

I stayed for a long time, looking through the books. Each one brought back a different memory of my grandpa and me, reading and talking together.

I also found some books that I'd never seen before. I was surprised to hear myself asking the lions, "Can I take some of these home?"

The lions looked solemnly at each other.

"That can be arranged," said Patience. "But first I need to get *you* back before dawn."

As we walked out of the library into the cold moonlight, Fortitude leaped onto an empty pedestal and lay down, staring straight ahead.

"Thank you for everything," I said.

"I hope to see you soon," he murmured.

In the wink of an eye, he turned to stone.

I stared, astounded. Then I remembered—Grandpa had once told me about the two famous lion statues that guarded the New York Public Library. I looked at Fortitude's grave marble face one last time. Then I climbed onto Patience's back, and we headed home.

When I woke up the next morning, my parents offered to return the book they had bought for me and get something else for my birthday.

"No," I said, "I want to keep it."

"What changed your mind?" asked my father.

"Well," I said, "mainly thinking about Grandpa."

I was pretty sure I had dreamed everything else.

Until I walked outside that morning. On
our doormat was a shiny new library card . . .

with some very big tooth marks.

Author's Note

For thousands of years, the builders of palaces and sacred temples have put pairs of lion statues at doorways to act as magical guardians. In 1910, the New York Public Library commissioned Edward Clark Potter to create lions for its main entrance. After much sketching in the Bronx Zoo, Potter sculpted a beautiful life-sized clay model. Then the six Piccirilli brothers worked in their Bronx studio to carve the statues from huge slabs of pink Tennessee marble.

During the Great Depression, New York City Mayor Fiorello LaGuardia named the statues Patience and Fortitude, after two key virtues useful for surviving hard times. New Yorkers quickly embraced them, and a longtime slogan of the New York Public Library was "Read Between the Lions." These days, the statues are much more than local icons, having become symbols for libraries around the world.

Of course, I didn't know any of this when I was a young boy first visiting New York City. The lions just seemed magical to me. Later, when I moved to New York after college, I would go to the public library for my dose of magic. And I still find it in every library I visit.

For Fiona and Naomi,
the magic in my life
—D.Z.

For Michele.
You teach your children well.
—R.C.

Visit us on the Web!
rhcbooks.com

Educators and librarians, for a variety of teaching tools, visit us at RHTeachersLibrarians.com

Library of Congress Cataloging-in-Publication Data is available upon request.
ISBN 978-1-5247-1798-8 (trade) — ISBN 978-1-5247-1799-5 (lib. bdg.) — ISBN 978-1-5247-1800-8 (ebook)

MANUFACTURED IN CHINA
10 9 8 7 6 5 4 3 2 1
First Edition

Random House Children's Books supports the First Amendment and celebrates the right to read.